Eileen Christelow

Five Little Monkeys

Looking for Santa

FOR
SANTA
AND
MRS CLAUS
♥ 5LM

CLARION BOOKS

Houghton Mifflin Harcourt · Boston · New York

Clump, clump, shuffle, creak . . .
Giggle . . . giggle . . .
SH-H-H-H! . . .

For Aidan and Kiri

Clarion Books
3 Park Avenue
New York, New York 10016

Copyright © 2021 by Eileen Christelow

All rights reserved. For information about permission
to reproduce selections from this book, write to
trade.permissions@hmhco.com or to Permissions,
Houghton Mifflin Harcourt Publishing Company,
3 Park Avenue, 19th Floor, New York, New York 10016.

Clarion Books is an imprint of
Houghton Mifflin Harcourt Publishing Company.

hmhbooks.com

The illustrations in this book were done
in Photoshop and Procreate.
The text was set in Cantoria MT Std.
The display text was set in FoldAndStaple BB.
Cover and Interior design by Stephanie Hays

Library of Congress Cataloging-in-Publication
Data is available.
ISBN 978-0-358-46985-8

Manufactured in China
SCP 10 9 8 7 6 5 4 3 2 1
4500823882

Do you hear that? What is going on?

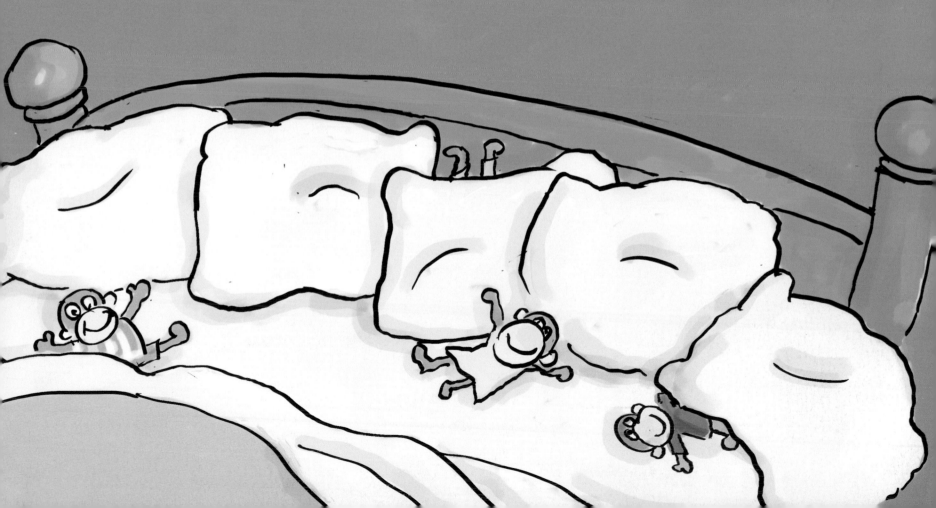

You guessed it!
It's the five little monkeys creeping
past Mama sleeping . . .

giggling, whispering,
sneaking down each stair.

Then there's a clatter
in the kitchen . . . **Clink . . . clickety, clack!** . . .

Could that be Santa, making a snack?

"Santa won't come while you're still awake. So go back to sleep, for goodness sake!"

Then a short time later, they hear . . . shuffle . . . shuffle . . . scuffle . . . in the hall and the squeak . . . click . . . of a door.

So of course those monkeys sneak out of bed once more!

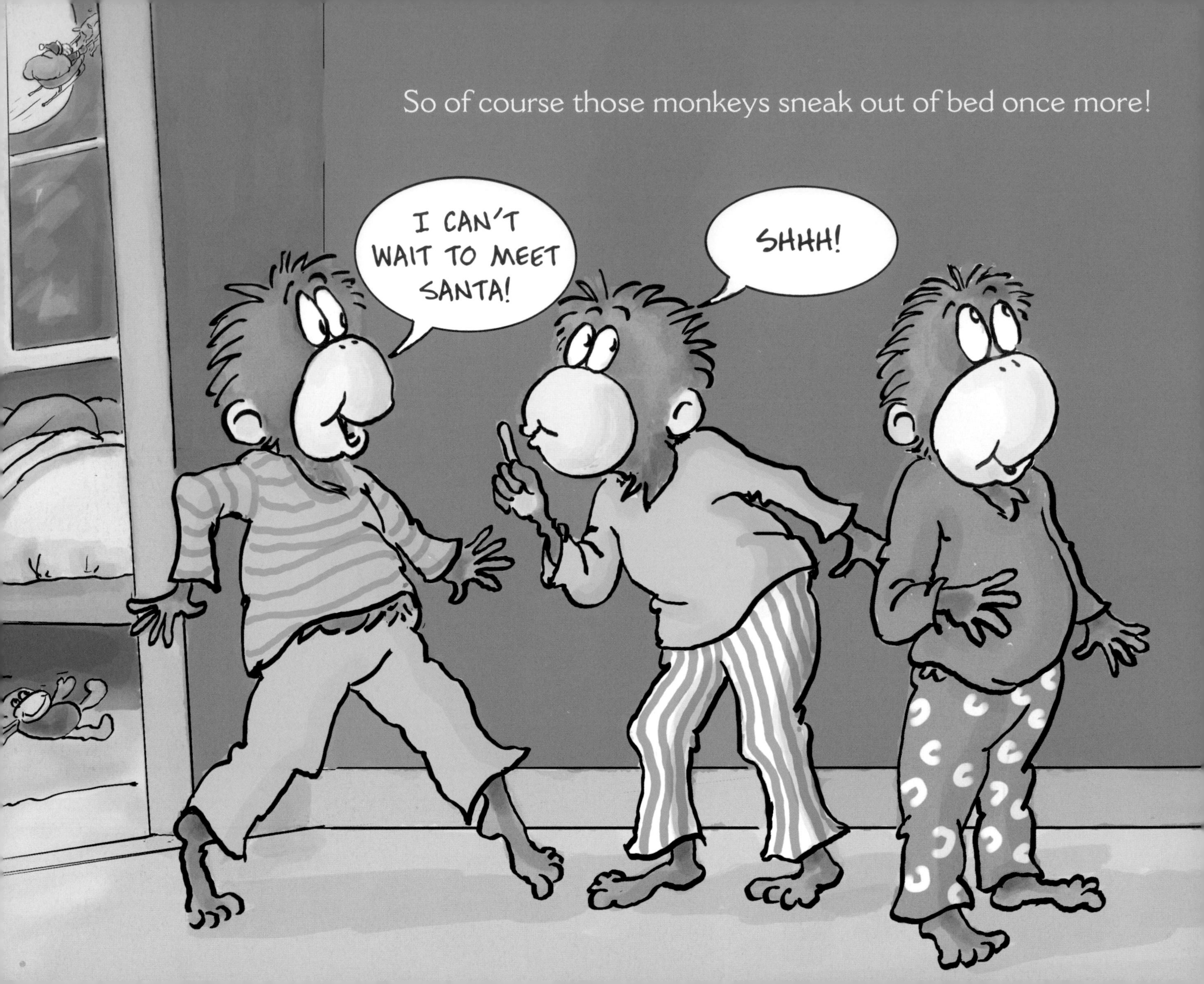

But when the door opens, it's Mama who's there.
"My goodness!" She gasps. "You gave me a scare!"

Of course those monkeys jump out of bed once more! They sneak down the stairs and out the front door.

The five little monkeys
find a ladder to climb.
Will Santa be there?
Let's hope so, this time!

But up on the roof, it's not Santa they see . . .
It's a thumping, bumping, broken branch of a tree.

Oh no!

Their ladder was
blown to the ground!

Now they're stuck on the roof . . . It can't be true!
And they're shivering cold. What can they do?

Five grimy monkeys land in a heap.
Grandpa is standing there.

"Why aren't you asleep?"

So they flop on the couch and soon start to snore.

Z-Z-Z-Z-Z-Z-Z-Z-Z-Z-Z-Z-Z-Z

Not a sound awakens them—
not anymore . . .

whoosh! . . . Thwump!

Not even munching and crunching and crinkling and crunkling!

But when there's a very quiet *squeak* . . . and a *click* . . .

. . . they're up in a flash! They need to be quick!

Santa is leaving! He's flying away!
They race outside in time to hear him say . . .

SANTA!

"Merry Christmas, little ones!

MERRY CHRISTMAS!

Now off to bed,
not one more peep.
Christmas will come sooner
If you go back to sleep!"